Pocket M

By Carmel Reilly

Illustrations by Adam Nickel

Chapter 1
A New Game

While Mara's mom looked at the paper and disks in the computer store, Mara looked at the games.

As she scanned the shelves, she recognized a game she wanted. She had played it before at her friend Kate's house, and although she knew it was quite difficult, she also knew it wouldn't be too hard for her.

Mara picked up the game and walked over to where her mother was standing.

"Mom, can I get this?" she asked.

Her mom took the box from Mara and turning it over, looked at the price.

"Oh," she said, "it's quite expensive. I think you might have to wait until your birthday to get this."

Mara was disappointed. "Mom, it's a long time until my birthday, and somebody else will probably buy it before then!" she said.

"What about the pocket money you've been saving?" asked Mom. "Perhaps you could use that."

"I don't think it'll be enough," answered Mara.

"You could always do some extra jobs. In that way, you'd save more quickly," suggested Mom. "I can think of some things for you to do at home, and you could try the neighbors, too. They might have some work for you."

Chapter 2
Helping Out

The following morning after breakfast Mara said, "Mom, have you organized any jobs for me to do?"

"Well," said Mom, "I spoke to Mrs. Joyce last night, and she told me that she would love some help cleaning her car. Would you like to do that?"

Mara thought about Mrs. Joyce, who lived by herself just down the street. Mrs. Joyce was very friendly, and she had a wonderful garden full of all kinds of trees, plants, and colorful flowers.

"Yes," Mara replied. "That sounds good."

Mrs. Joyce was standing next to her car in the driveway
as Mara came in the gate.

"Thank you so much for coming over," Mrs. Joyce said
cheerfully. "Washing the car isn't a really hard job, but at
my age, I find it's much easier when I have somebody
young like you to help me out."

Mrs. Joyce had two buckets ready. One was full of warm, soapy water for washing, and the other was full of cool clear water for rinsing. She gave Mara a cloth, and together, they started work.

9

Chapter 3

Leaving Early

Mara was kneeling down cleaning the side of the car, when she heard a voice she knew. She looked up to see her friend Kate leaning against the gate.

"Hello," said Kate. "Your mom told me you were here. Do you want to come over to my house? We can play on the computer, and Dad says when we get tired of that, he'll take us to the park."

"That sounds good," replied Mara, "but I'm helping Mrs. Joyce."

"Couldn't you leave a little early?" asked Kate.

Mara wasn't sure if she should leave. She looked over at Mrs. Joyce. "Do you still need my help?" she asked. "Would it be all right if I left now?"

"Yes, I can finish this by myself," Mrs. Joyce answered. "Off you go."

Although Mrs. Joyce was smiling, Mara thought she looked slightly disappointed.

When Kate and Mara were together, they usually couldn't stop talking, but today as they walked up the street to Kate's house, they were almost silent.

"Are you all right?" Kate asked Mara. "You're so quiet today."

"I was thinking about Mrs. Joyce. Perhaps I shouldn't have left her to do all that work by herself," replied Mara.

"I'm sure Mrs. Joyce will be fine," said Kate. "Anyway, you can always go back later when we've finished our game."

"But she won't need help then," said Mara. "She needs help now."

As they approached Kate's house, Kate said, "My brother won't be back for hours, so we can play the new computer game for as long as we like."

"That's what I'm supposed to be working for," said Mara. "I was going to buy that game with the money I'm saving – but it doesn't look like I'm going to be saving very much if I don't do any work."

Chapter 4
Finishing the Job

Kate started to walk inside her house. "Come on," she said. "You're here now, so let's just have some fun. You can think about saving later."

Mara stood on Kate's front doorstep looking rather unhappy. "I have to go back," she said. "It's not really the pocket money. It's the fact that I promised Mrs. Joyce I would help, and she was relying on me. I did the wrong thing, and I feel terrible."

Kate nodded and began to say something, but Mara had already turned and was running back down the street.

"Oh, hello," said Mrs. Joyce, surprised to see Mara again so soon.

"I've come to finish the job," said Mara as she walked toward the car. "I decided that I can play that game anytime, but you need my help right now."

As Mara picked up the cloth, Mrs. Joyce said, "You're right, and I'm very glad to see you back."